Dear mouse friends,
Welcome to the world of

Geronimo Stilton

THE RODENT'S GAZETTE
EDITORIAL STAFF

Geronimo Stilton
A learned and brainy
mouse; editor of
The Rodent's Gazette

Thea Stilton
Geronimo's sister and
special correspondent at
The Rodent's Gazette

Trap Stilton
An awful joker;
Geronimo's cousin and
owner of the store
Cheap Junk for Less

Benjamin Stilton
A sweet and loving
nine-year-old mouse;
Geronimo's favorite
nephew

Geronimo Stilton

A VERY MERRY CHRISTMAS

Scholastic Inc.

New York   Toronto   London   Auckland   Sydney
Mexico City   New Delhi   Hong Kong   Buenos Aires

ISBN 978-0-545-02135-7

Based on an original idea by Elisabetta Dami.

www.geronimostilton.com

Published by Scholastic Inc., 557 Broadway, New York, NY 10012. SCHOLASTIC and associated logos are trademarks and/or registered trademarks of Scholastic Inc.

Text by Geronimo Stilton
Original title Inseguimento a New York
Cover by Giuseppe Ferrario
Illustrations by Claudius Cernuschi, Giuseppe Di Dio, and Christian Aliprandi
Graphics by Merenguita Gingermouse and Yuko Egusa

Special thanks to Beth Dunfey
Translated by Lidia Morson Tramontozzi
Interior design by Kay Petronio

12   12 13 14 15 16/0

Printed in the U.S.A.   40
First printing, September 2008

CHRISTMASTIME IS ALWAYS SPECIAL

It was winter in New Mouse City, the capital of Mouse Island, and the weather outside was FRIGHTFUL. Sitting at my desk one chilly evening, I gazed out my WINDOW at the snowflakes falling softly over the city.

Oh, I almost forgot to introduce myself! My name is Stilton, *Geronimo Stilton*.

I'm the publisher of *The Rodent's Gazette*, the most famouse newspaper here on Mouse Island.

I shivered and put my paws up on the space heater I kept under my desk. Sometimes it felt as if winter would go on forever. **Brrrrr!** I hate cold weather.

But then I remembered something that cheered me up. CHRISTMAS was just a few days away!

Ah, Christmas! It was my *favorite* holiday.

Just thinking about Christmas reminded me of all the things I had to do. Holey cheese, my list was almost as long as Santa's! I still had to DECORATE my mouse hole, buy last-minute GIFTS, and figure out the holiday menu. There were so many delicious treats to eat at Christmastime — candy canes, roasted chestnuts, toasted cheese logs . . .

VISIONS OF
CHEESE PUFFS

As I sat there *daydreaming* about the **magic** of Christmas, the door burst open and my grandfather **William Shortpaws** stomped in. He shoved his snout within an inch of mine and shouted,

"WAAAAAAAAAAAAAAAKE UP!

Are there visions of cheese puffs dancing in your head, Grandson?! WAKE UP!"

I almost **JUMPED OUT** of my fur. "No, of course not. Well . . . what do you mean by '**VISIONS** of cheese puffs'? I was thinking about the menu for **CHRISTMAS** dinner, and cheese puffs would certainly be delicious."

"I know it's almost Christmas, but that's no

excuse for DAYDREAMING!" Grandfather thundered. "Geronimo, I want you to focus on business. On the newspaper! It doesn't run itself, you know! This paper needs a leader with NEW IDEAS, not one who naps on the job!"

He pointed to a  that hung from the wall. It said:

THE WISE
MOUSE WASTES
NEITHER TIME
NOR CHEESE!

Then he **tapped** his paw on my snout a couple of times. "**Knock, knock, anybody home?**"

He picked up the phone and called Miss Raven, one of the assistants on staff. He boomed, "Miss Raven, please send a *memo* to everybody at *The Rodent's Gazette*: THE WISE MOUSE WASTES NEITHER TIME NOR CHEESE! *Sign it*: William Shortpaws."

I sighed. "Don't get your tail in a twist, Grandfather. Even if you don't sign it, everyone will know the memo comes from you." It was true. No one else would be so obnoxious!

"Well, if I didn't pop in from time to time to see how things are going, this paper would be about as successful as moldy cheese at an early-rat special." Grandfather SNiFFeD. Suddenly, he brightened up. "Oh, I almost forgot what I came here to tell you. I had a great idea!"

Uh-oh. That made me a little worried. You see, my grandfather really was a brilliant mouse. But his great ideas **always** seemed to get me into trouble. "You had a great idea?" I repeated nervously.

"Yes!" he exclaimed. "This year, the entire Stilton family will spend CHRISTMAS . . ."

He paused and gave me a sly look. I knew he was just trying to make the moment more dramatic, but the anticipation was DRIVING ME CRAZY!

"Where, Grandfather?"

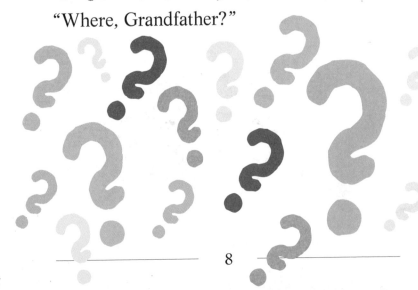

New York?
Why New York?

"**New York**? Why New York?" I asked.

Grandfather smiled. "Because my best friend, **Klondyke MacMouse**, lives in New York! I met him a long time ago when traveling around the world for *The Rodent's Gazette*. Which reminds me, Grandson, you should be out there sniffing out new stories instead of in here **warming** your tail in that cushy chair!"

I opened my mouth to defend myself, but before I could squeak a word, Grandfather cut me off. "Well anyway, Klondyke invited us to spend Christmas with his family. He lives in a fantastic apartment overlooking CENTRAL PARK."

Dear Willy,

How are you? I was thinking about all the fabumouse times we used to have when you were the editor of <u>The Rodent's Gazette</u>. Every so often, you'd pop up in New York looking for a scoop to jazz up your newspaper. We used to go out and see all the sights! Ah, to be young in New York . . .

I got to thinking: We may be getting older, and our whiskers may be falling out, but we can still have a good time! So I'd like to invite you and your entire family to spend Christmas at my home here in New York City. I hope you'll accept the invitation of a dear old friend.

Yours truly,
Klondyke MacMouse

He waved a *letter* and a **PHOTO** under my snout.

"But, Grandfather, we always celebrate Christmas at my mouse hole in New Mouse City!" I protested. "It's **TRADITION**! We've been doing it for years."

Grandfather snorted. "Geronimo, traditions are made to be broken. Besides, you always say that it's exciting to discover different *customs* and *cultures* and to have new EXPE RIE*n*CEs!"

Thousands of faces and traditions in one world!

I twitched my tail anxiously. He had a good point there. "You're right, Grandfather," I said. "But maybe we should have Christmas at my place and *then* we can travel — "

Grandfather William cut me off. "Nothing doing, Geronimo. It's all **arranged**. The rest of the **family** has already agreed to go to New York."

My whiskers **drooped**. "Really?" I couldn't believe no one had told me. I was always the last to know the **BIG** family news. "Well, of course, if everyone else wants to go, then there's nothing to squeak about."

Suddenly the door burst open and the entire **family** raced into my office.

"Uncle Geronimo, did you hear?" my nephew Benjamin squealed. "We're spending **CHRISTMAS** in New York! We're all *LEAVING* tomorrow!"

Grandma Honeywhisker

Grandpa Longwhisker

Uncle Grayfur

Aunt Sweetfur

Geronimo

Grandfather William Shortpaws

Cindy Shirley

A traditional Christmas at Geronimo's house

I smiled down at my favorite nephew and tried to sound **EnthUsIAstIC**. "Yes, yes, Grandfather just told me. We'll spend Christmas in New York. It'll be great!"

Everybody was excited. They were all **squeaking** at once, happily making plans for the trip. As for myself, I started for home.

That night, I went to bed early. I was **depressed**. You see, I was worried that I

hadn't **orgαNized** fun Christmases at my mouse hole. That had to be the reason everyone was so excited to spend Christmas in New York.

Maybe my **cooking** wasn't tasty enough for the family gourmets.

Maybe my **decorations** weren't creative enough for the family artists.

Maybe my gifts weren't **fun** enough for the family mouselings.

Yes, it was all my fault everyone wanted to go to New York for Christmas instead of spending it at our **beloved** home in New Mouse City. I had been a terrible host. And I had no one but myself to blame.

I lay awake for a very long time, feeling **MISERABLE**. Finally, I curled up into a fur ball and fell asleep.

A TRIP TO THE BIG APPLE*

The next day, the entire Stilton family left for New York. Everyone except me, that is. I stayed behind until two days before Christmas. I had **SO MUCH WORK** to do at the newspaper that I just couldn't tear myself away before then.

On my last afternoon in the office, I wished my coworkers a Merry Christmas. Then I hurried home to prepare for the trip. I put my best suit in my yellow **suitcase**. Then I packed all the 🅖 🅘 🅕 🅣 🅢 my grandfather had bought for the MacMouse family. "Grandson, I want to make a **nice** impression on the MacMouses," he'd shouted at me. "So don't forget anything!" I didn't. I was

*"Big Apple" is an expression used to describe New York City.

too scared of him to leave anything behind!

Last but not least, I attached a bright BLUE TAG with my name and address to the suitcase handle. That would make it easier for me to find it when I arrived in New York.

I scurried to the airport and turned in my bag at the check-in counter. The agent took it with a smile. "You can pick up your luggage in New York, Mr. Stilton. No need to worry."

I thanked him and headed to the gate, where my plane was waiting. Half an hour later, I BOARDED the plane and my trip was under way.

I settled into my seat and pulled out a tourist guide to New York. Then I got out a map of the city and looked for the MacMouses' house.

THE TALE OF NEW YORK

New York City, also known as the **Big Apple**, is one of the biggest cities in the world. Many consider it the center of business and finance, entertainment and fashion, and media and education. The Lenape inhabited the region when the Europeans began to explore the area in 1524. The Italian navigator **Giovanni da Verrazzano** was the first European to enter New York Bay. Then in1625, Dutch fur merchants formed a settlement called New Amsterdam as the main town of their colony, New Netherland.

In 1664, the English conquered the colony and renamed it New York in honor of the Duke of York, the future King James II.

From 1785 to 1790, New York City was the capital of the United States. It was also the capital of New York State until 1797.

Today, this great metropolis is an important world **financial center**, and it is the biggest city in the United States. It is also one of the most popular tourist spots in the world.

PLACES OF INTEREST IN N.Y.

New York City is made up of five boroughs: Manhattan, the Bronx, Brooklyn, Queens, and Staten Island. Manhattan, the island between the Hudson River and the East River, is the heart of the city. It has the most famouse and interesting places to visit, including Central Park, the Metropolitan Museum of Art and, of course, Times Square.

It's very easy to get around in New York City. Manhattan looks like a big, long checkerboard. It has great big streets and avenues. **A Native American trail** that cut through the island is still in existence. It is now called **Broadway**.

Manhattan is home to some of the tallest **skyscrapers** in the world. This is possible thanks to the composition of its subsoil, which is made of hard granite capable of sustaining immense weight without sinking.

More than **eight million** people from more than 185 different countries live in New York City. They are Africans, Hispanics, Italians, Irish, Chinese, etc. More than 130 different languages are spoken in New York.

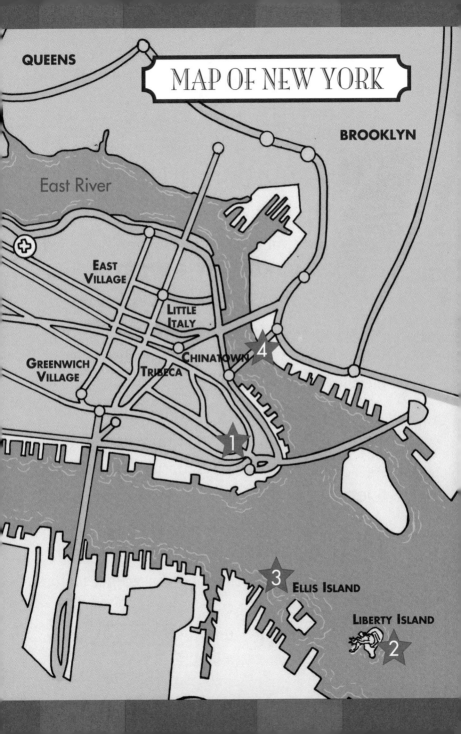

A Yellow Bag with a Bright Blue Tag

After a long, bumpy flight, we finally landed at New York's **KENNEDY AIRPORT**. And not a moment too soon, as far as I was concerned! My paws were so **CRAMPED** and STIFF, I felt like I'd been stuffed inside a tin of miniature cheese snacks.

It was morning. The airport was already crowded and incredibly busy. There were tons of rodents scurrying about **all over the place**. Some had just arrived and others were about to depart. Everyone was in a hurry to get somewhere.

After waiting in the long line to get to the immigration counter to have my passport stamped, I headed for the **BAGGAGE** claim area to retrieve my suitcase from **MOUSE AIR**, the official airline of Mouse Island.

I couldn't wait to get my bag.

I was already looking forward to a nice warm **bath** and something **CHEESY** to munch on at the MacMouses' apartment. I was so tired from the long flight, I felt like I was going to fall asleep on my paws. I kept **YAWNING**.

Then I **SAW** a **yellow** bag with a **BRIGHT BLUE** tag on the baggage carousel, and I got a second wind. I grabbed it and headed for the exit.

At the check-in counter, I check my yellow bag with Mouse Air.

There's my bag on the conveyor belt. It's about to be loaded onto the airplane that will take me to New York.

At 9:00 P.M., my plane takes off.

THIS ISN'T MY BAG!

Outside the airport, it was snowing! I hailed a **taxi**. Then I loaded my suitcase into the trunk and gave the driver the MacMouses' address in Manhattan.

Halfway into the city, I realized I didn't have my *wallet* on me. Holey cheese, I only had my passport and the New York City tourist guide in my pocket! I must have left my wallet in my suitcase.

I asked the cabdriver to *pull over*. He popped the trunk and I took out the yellow bag.

When I opened it, I had a big *surprise*.

Crusty kitty litter, this wasn't my bag! Where were all my clothes? The Christmas gifts for the MacMouses were missing! If I

didn't find those gifts, I'd be **cheese toast**. Grandfather William would make sure of it.

"Oh, no! This isn't my bag!" I cried.

The cabdriver shrugged. "That's your problem, not mine. I just want my **MONEY**!"

"But . . . but . . . I don't have a penny on me. My wallet is in my bag!" I shrieked.

Since I didn't have any money, the cabbie demanded my beloved *gold fountain pen* as payment. I didn't dare complain. He was so huge he looked like a sumo rat, with massive **muscles** that looked even bigger when he was mad.

He snatched the pen from my paw and climbed back in the cab, **slamming** the door behind him.

The cab **ZOOMED** away, leaving **SKID MARKS** behind it. It wasn't until it had disappeared from sight that I realized I was stranded on the highway!

I stood on the side of the road in the snow. I was halfway between the airport and Manhattan. I was miles from home. I was exhausted. I had no money. I had a **HUMONGOUS** bag to lug around — and it wasn't even mine!

MRS. SMITH'S SUITCASE

I sat at the edge of the highway. I couldn't even make a phone call. I'd left my cell phone inside my bag. I wanted to CRY.

But I stood up and straightened my tail. There was only one thing to do — I had to get that bag back to its **owner** and hope that he or she had my bag. It couldn't be that hard, could it?

I took a better look at the bag. It was yellow, just like mine, with a bright blue tag, just like mine. The tag had a name on it: **MRS. A. Smith**.

MOLDY MOZZARELLA . . . Smith?! That had to be the most common name in New York City. There were bound to be hundreds of Smiths!

Inside the suitcase there were **DRESSES**, *makeup*, and panty hose. There were also lots of books and several notebooks filled with notes on ancient Egypt, plus an X-ray of a **MUMMY**. The rodent who had taken my luggage was an Egyptologist — that is, someone who studies ancient Egyptian civilization.

MRS. A. Smith

Suddenly, I heard ringing from inside the bag.

Ring ring! Ring ring! Ring ring!

I grabbed the bag and started digging through it. At the very bottom was a CELL PHONE. Could the rodent whose bag I'd TAKEN by accident be calling me? There was only one way to find out!

I answered the phone. "Hello, is this Mrs. Smith? This is Stilton, *Geronimo Stilton*."

"Yes, this is Mrs. Smith," a female mouse's voice replied.

"I have your bag," I informed her. Well, she probably realized that . . . how else could I have answered her **phone**?

"And I have yours!" she chimed. "I'll meet you at Columb . . ."

Rat-munching rattlesnakes! The phone had gone DEAD.

Mrs. Smith's bag

Tears of frustration and exhaustion rolled down my snout. As you know, dear reader, I've had a lot of **ADVENTURES**. But this was turning out to be the most unlucky one yet.

After a moment or two, I wiped my eyes. Then I started GOING THROUGH Mrs. Smith's bag. I felt guilty — I never look through other mice's things. But this was different. It was an *EMERGENCY*!

In one of the side pockets, I found something that might help me: Mrs. Smith's appointment book. This is what she had Planned for the day.

Hmmmm. When the phone cut off, Mrs. Smith was saying "Columb . . ." She must have been saying **COLUMBIA UNIVERSITY**. She had an appointment there at ten o'clock! If I got there in time, maybe we could exchange

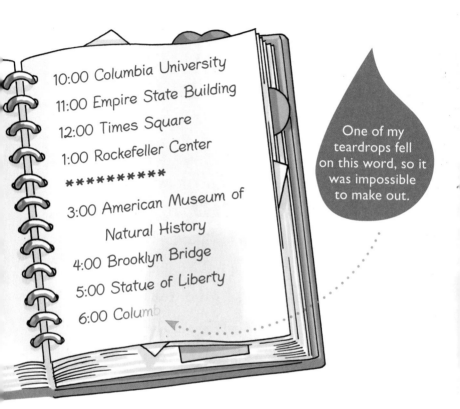

10:00 Columbia University
11:00 Empire State Building
12:00 Times Square
1:00 Rockefeller Center
****
3:00 American Museum of
Natural History
4:00 Brooklyn Bridge
5:00 Statue of Liberty
6:00 Columb

One of my teardrops fell on this word, so it was impossible to make out.

B A G S. Then I'd get the MacMouses' Christmas gifts back, and Grandfather would never have to know what had happened.

Well, was I a *millipede* or a mouse? I could do it. I had to!

HEADLIGHTS
IN THE FOG

Shivering from the cold, I put one paw in front of the other. I had to get to Manhattan.

Cars **WHIZZED** by me, coming a little closer than I liked. Rodents here seemed to drive much faster than they did in New Mouse City. In the morning fog, the yellow headlights glimmered like cats' eyes. **It was terrifying.**

But cold and miserable as I was, I was still fascinated by what I saw around me. New York was truly an extraordinary place! The city never slept. It was in a state of constant motion.

The snow had stopped. I dragged the yellow bag behind me like a sack of moldy **CHEESE RINDS**. It left a trail through the

brown slush on the side of the road.

I kept slipping, but I continued on my way. What else could I do?

I considered going to the MacMouses for help, but I was too embarrassed. "No way can I tell Grandfather I lost those gifts!" I panted as I stepped into a puddle of slush. "My fur will be gray and patchy before I hear the end of it!"

When I got to Manhattan, I looked like I'd gone paw-to-claw with an oversized tabby. I was **COVERED WITH MUD** from snout to shoe. I was soaked to the bone. I felt as if I hadn't slept in a week. I hadn't eaten in hours, and I didn't have a penny to my name. My map was so wet and dirty it was falling apart.

But as I looked around me, I couldn't help thinking, *Holey cheese, what a beautiful city!*

Too Many Smiths!

I started walking uptown. I still didn't have a cent for the subway. It was just my luck that Columbia was at the northern end of Manhattan . . . and I was at the southern end.

But when I finished the long trek, it was worth it. What a gorgeous university! Everywhere I looked, there were students bustling about. They looked so studious — and so serious!

I turned to a mouse with fur the color of ebony and said, "Good morning, Miss. May I ask you a question?"

"Of course," she answered pleasantly. "I'm not quite sure if I can help you, but try me. I'm a professor here. What would you like to know?"

COLUMBIA UNIVERSITY

Columbia University was founded in 1754 as King's College by the order of King George II of England. It is one of the oldest and most prestigious universities in America. Today, it is mostly known for its schools of law, medicine, and journalism.

"Well, I'm looking for Mrs. Smith," I began.

The professor laughed. "S M I T H? Do you realize that's the most common name in the United States?"

"Uh, yes," I answered.

"Tell me her first name," the professor suggested. "Maybe that will help."

"I don't know it," I confessed. "I only know that it starts with an **A**."

She shook her head. "Like Anna? Or Anastasia? How about Anita? Or Ada? Maybe Adelaide? Have you any idea how many A. Smiths there are at this university? Where are you from? I can tell you're not a New Yorker!"

"Yes, I know it's going to be hard finding her," I mumbled. "You see, I was at the airport, and I took her bag by accident. She has my bag with all my MONEY and my cell phone. I haven't slept . . . or washed . . . or eaten . . ." It was then that I started sobbing. I tried to stop myself, but I couldn't. I was just so tired.

The professor took pity on me. She offered me a **CUP** of hot cheese and pointed me to a bathroom where I could WASH my paws and face. Before she said good-bye, she gave me a new map of the city.

"Good luck finding her," she said. "You'll need it!"

I looked over Mrs. Smith's appointment book and decided to look for her at her next appointment: eleven o'clock at the **EMPIRE STATE BUILDING**. Unfortunately, it was nowhere near Columbia. How was I ever going to get there on time? I had only an hour and lots of ground to cover.

UP, UP, UP IN THE EMPIRE STATE BUILDING

I walked and walked. It seemed like I'd be walking forever. My paws were so cold and sore they'd gone numb.

Just when I thought I couldn't take another step, I saw a **skateboard** peeking out of a garbage can. That gave me a BRiLLiaNt idea!

I put the skateboard on the ground and placed one paw on it to see if it would **hold**. "Hmm, I could probably use this..." I muttered.

But I didn't get a chance to finish my thought. Another rodent on the sidewalk accidentally BUMPED into me, and the next thing I knew, I was *RACING* along

like a hamster on a treadmill.

I zoomed through the crowds of New York, screaming, "HELP! GET OUT OF THE WAAAAY!"

I was whizzing down **BROADWAY**, the biggest and most famous street in all of New York. The street seemed to go on forever!

At last I came to **34th Street**. Somehow I managed to hang a left. Now I was speeding toward Fifth Avenue. I skidded to a halt.

Phew! I had made it to the Empire State Building without a scratch.

EMPIRE STATE BUILDING

1,454 FEET HIGH

6,500 WINDOWS

103 FLOORS

SPEED OF ELEVATOR: 600 TO 1,000 FEET PER MINUTE

73 ELEVATORS

410 DAYS TO BUILD IT

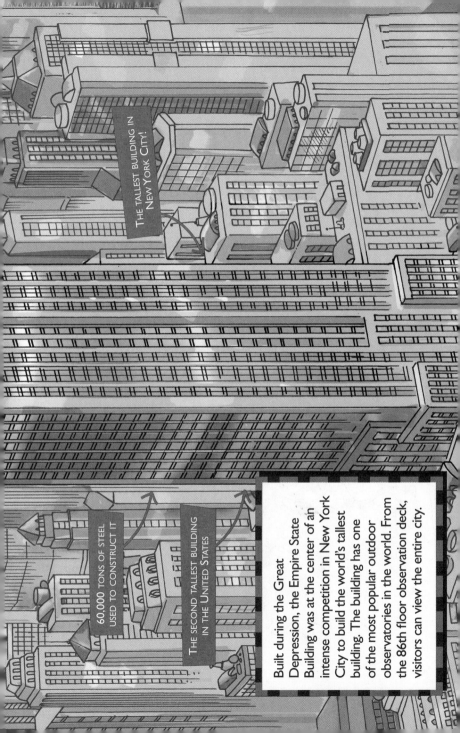

THE TALLEST BUILDING IN NEW YORK CITY!

60,000 TONS OF STEEL USED TO CONSTRUCT IT

THE SECOND TALLEST BUILDING IN THE UNITED STATES

Built during the Great Depression, the Empire State Building was at the center of an intense competition in New York City to build the world's tallest building. The building has one of the most popular outdoor observatories in the world. From the 86th floor observation deck, visitors can view the entire city.

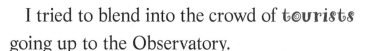
I tried to blend into the crowd of **tourists** going up to the Observatory.

The elevator took us up, up, up to the **86**th floor. We went so high I could feel my ears popping. Cheese niblets! I hate heights.

But when I scurried out onto the observation deck, I was **stunned**. The view left me absolutely breathless. What a magnificent **panorama** of the city!

Unfortunately, I didn't have time to stop and enjoy the **sights**. I had to look for Mrs. Smith. I saw a mouse with a green jacket and asked, **"Excuse me, are you Mrs. Smith?"**

She **SHOOK** her snout.

The next rodent I asked **pinched** my

cheek. "No, I'm not Mrs. Smith, but if you want to call me that you can, my little **cutie-patootie**!"

"I-I-I'm sorry," I stammered. "There's been a mistake."

There had to be a faster way to find her. So I took a deep breath and shouted, "**Mrs. Smith!!!!!!!!!!!!!**"

Everybody stared at me. I could hear them murmuring,

"You can tell he's not a New Yorker!"

A security guard grabbed me by the ear and dragged me downstairs.

WATCH THE TAIL!

I pulled out Mrs. Smith's appointment book, then looked at my **watch**. The next appointment was at noon in TIMES SQUARE. If I hurried, I could still make it! I was too fond of my fur to set a paw on that skateboard again. Fortunately for my sore paws, Times Square was not too far from the Empire State Building. I soon found myself in a beautiful square filled with neon lights, billboards, SKYSCRAPERS, and theater marquees. Holey cheese! The square was so bright, I wished I had sunglasses!

I stood still for a moment, trying to catch my breath. I was right outside a fancy hotel with big GLASS doors. Suddenly, two rodents with smart blue uniforms came

TIMES SQUARE

Times Square is a crossroads of theaters, restaurants, and skyscrapers. It was originally called Longacre Square. The name was changed in 1904, when *The New York Times*, the most famouse newspaper in the United States, moved its headquarters to the square.

rushing out. As they **unrolled** a long **RED CARPET**, they shouted to each other, "Hurry up, will you? She's coming!"

I tried asking, "She? Who's com . . . ?"

But the carpet knocked me right off my paws!

I found myself snout-down on the pavement as the two doormice rolled the **CARPET** right over my back!

A *beautiful* blond rodent stepped out of a **LONG**, shiny *limousine*. Within seconds, a huge crowd had formed.

"That's her. It's really her! MOUSELINA!" someone shouted.

The rodent walked slowly along the red carpet, smiling and signing *autographs*. She was about to step on me, so I said, **"Watch the tail!"**

I meant my tail, but she looked behind her and saw that the tail of her long, *elegant* gown was caught in the door of the limousine. She smiled and planted a kiss on my cheek. Then she gave me the red *rose* she was holding. "Thank you. You're my hero!"

WHAT PUSHY PAWS!

In seconds, the crowd was swarming all over me like a pack of hungry rats at an **all-you-can-eat** cheese buffet. Everyone was trying to grab my rose.

"IT'S MINE! I SAW IT FIRST! I'M HER BIGGEST FAN! IT'S MINE!" they squealed.

I had to protect myself. These New York mice were such pushy paws! So I let the two doormice roll me up in carpet. Then they took me safely into the hotel.

As I scrambled out, I could hear the crowd muttering **angrily**.

I didn't have time to worry about what a bunch of crazy raterazzi thought of me. I was a mouse on a mission! But I realized that in all the confusion, I'd missed my chance to find Mrs. Smith. Cheese slices! Locating Mrs. Smith was turning out to be as easy as tracking down the latest Ratendo game on Christmas Eve! If I had any hope of finding her I'd have to hurry to her next appointment: one o'clock at ROCKEFELLER CENTER.

I was late! I raced along like I had a HUNGRY cat at my heels. My paws ached. My back was sore. And my heart was beating so fast it sounded like one of those bongo drummers back in Times Square. Even so, I arrived at Rockefeller Center

ROCKEFELLER CENTER

Rockefeller Center is a city within a city.
This building complex has gardens, stores,
restaurants, and offices. It's also home to the
biggest Christmas tree in all of New York.
The tree is lit right after Thanksgiving to kick
off the holiday season.

ten minutes late! Panting, I collapsed on top of Mrs. Smith's yellow bag. I had to sit down before my paws gave out.

When I looked up, I saw the hugest, most *fabumouse* Christmas tree ever. It was set above a **BEAUTIFUL** skating rink crowded with rodents of every age, shape, and fur color. They were all bundled up in heavy parkas and *colorful* hats.

"Mrs. Smith, are you here?" I shouted to the crowd. "Mrs. Smith?" No one answered.

THE FRIGHT OF A LIFETIME!

I looked at my watch. It was later than I'd thought. Mrs. Smith must already be on her way to her next appointment: two o'clock at the **AMERICAN MUSEUM OF NATURAL HISTORY**.

I sighed and picked up the yellow bag. Then, with my head hanging and my tail dragging between my legs, I headed toward the museum.

When I arrived, I realized I had a **BIG** problem. I didn't have any **MONEY** for the entrance fee! I almost cried.

But then I caught a break. Right near the museum's front door stood a cleaning cart. I hid the bag behind a PLANT, then

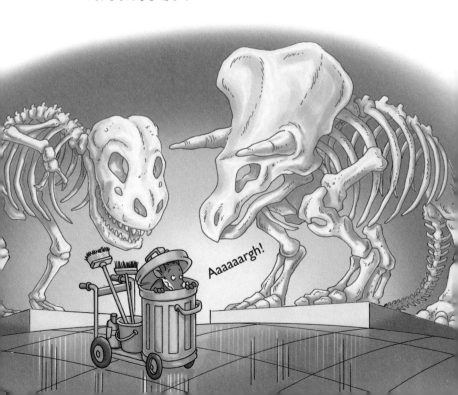

SCRAMBLED inside the garbage can. A few moments later, a cleaning mouse wheeled me inside the museum.

I waited patiently while we clattered along. Then, as soon as it was safe to stick my snout out of the bin, I took a peek outside . . . and got the fright of my life!

An ENORMOUSE skull was staring at me!

Aaaaaargh!

It was the hugest **dinosaur** skeleton I had ever seen! I screeched and *SCURRIED* out of the garbage can.

I scrambled into the next room and raised my head to see an enormouse **WHALE** that looked as if it was about to fall on top of me! I just couldn't take it any more — not in my weakened, hungry state. I FAINTED.

A member of the museum staff revived me with extra-stinky-smelling cheeses.

"Are you **okay**, sir?" she asked.

I nodded weakly.

"Some mice do find our dinosaur bones and model whale a little overwhelming," she said kindly.

Dinosaur bones? Model whale? Of course! This was a natural history museum, after all. I should have realized they weren't real.

Help!

No Sleep Till the Brooklyn Bridge

I didn't know if I could go on. I was exhausted. But I couldn't give up now. I had to prove myself. If I didn't get those G I F T S back, Grandfather would never let me forget it!

I retrieved the yellow bag and strode out of the museum with my snout **held high**. I checked the time. I could still make it to the next appointment if I hurried.

I hailed a taxi and offered the driver my *gold watch* in exchange for a ride to the **BROOKLYN BRIDGE**.

"And step on it! I'm in a hurry!" I told him.

The cabdriver took off like a cat burglar

fleeing the scene of a crime. "**HEEERE WE GOOOOOOOOOOO!**" he shouted.

I felt like I was trapped in a *RATRACER* 3000 videogame!

After ten minutes, I was as PALE as death.

After twenty minutes, I was as green as broccoli.

After thirty minutes, I rolled down the window and lost my cheese!
AURGH-ACK!

Thanks to the cabbie's **c r a z y** driving, we had already arrived at the **BROOKLYN BRIDGE**.

After 10 minutes . . .

After 20 minutes . . .

After 30 minutes . . .

Today the Brooklyn Bridge is the second busiest bridge in New York City. Every day, 144,000 vehicles cross the bridge!

Each thick steel cable has 5,434 wires that have been twisted together for extra strength. These specially designed cables can withstand strong winds, rain, and snow.

The bridge weighs 14,680 tons.

BROOKLYN BRIDGE

The Brooklyn Bridge opened in 1883. It was designed by the German-born architect John A. Roebling. It connects Manhattan to Brooklyn. When the bridge was built, the two boroughs were separate cities. The Brooklyn Bridge was the first suspension bridge to use steel for its cable wire.

What a *magnificent* sight! It was the most beautiful bridge I'd ever seen. It was easy to understand why it was so famouse.

As I headed toward the pedestrian path, I noticed the long steel cables supporting the bridge. It was terrifying! "What if one of the support **CABLES** snaps?" I thought, getting panicky. "What if one of the PILINGS crumbles? What if a *HURRICANE* comes sweeping by?"

I couldn't take it anymore. I screamed at the top of my lungs, **"Mrs. Smith, where are you???"**

All the rodents on the bridge stared at me disapprovingly.

Fortunately for me, a big group of **TOURISTS** arrived at that exact moment. Desperate to avoid the **STARES** of everyone around me, I hustled into the middle of their group. I was so humiliated, I'd turned **red** from the tip of my snout to the end of my tail. In fact, I think I'd set a new world record for most embarrassing moments in a single day.

Oh, how I *wished* I was back in my nice cozy mouse hole with a nice cup of hot cheese by my side!

LADY LIBERTY

For once on this awful day, I had a stroke of luck. The tourists were heading toward the ferry that sailed to the Statue of Liberty. That was where Mrs. Smith was heading for her next appointment!

But of course, I still didn't have any money to pay my fare. All I had in my pocket was a button and an old crust of cheese.

So I went to the ferry's captain, a **huge** rodent with paws as big as a cat's, and told him I didn't have money for a ticket, but that I desperately needed to get to Liberty Island.

The captain looked at me appraisingly. "You don't, huh? Well, well! Let's see what we can do with you." The captain rubbed his paws together in anticipation.

"I've got it! Take that oversized mop and start **scrubbing** the deck! Make it shine! If I'm totally **satisfied**, I'll pay for your ticket to get into the STATUE OF LIBERTY!" He smiled down at me. "Today's your lucky day!"

"I'll do it," I told the captain. I picked up the mop and began to swab the deck.

A few minutes later, I looked up from my work. There she was! The famous **LADY LIBERTY** was emerging through the fog.

THE STATUE OF LIBERTY
The Statue of Liberty is a symbol of freedom for millions of people. The artist Frédéric-Auguste Bartholdi sculpted the statue; the interior was engineered by Gustave Eiffel, the designer of the Eiffel Tower. The people of France donated the statue to the people of the United States in 1886 to commemorate 100 years of American independence.

THE TABLET LADY LIBERTY HOLDS IS INSCRIBED "JULY 4, 1776," WITH THE NUMBERS IN ROMAN NUMERALS — THE DAY THE UNITED STATES DECLARED ITS INDEPENDENCE FROM ENGLAND.

THE SEVEN RAYS IN THE CROWN REPRESENT THE SEVEN SEAS AND THE SEVEN CONTINENTS —ASIA, EUROPE, AFRICA, AUSTRALIA, NORTH AMERICA, ANTARCTICA, AND SOUTH AMERICA.

THE TORCH SYMBOLIZES ENLIGHTENMENT.

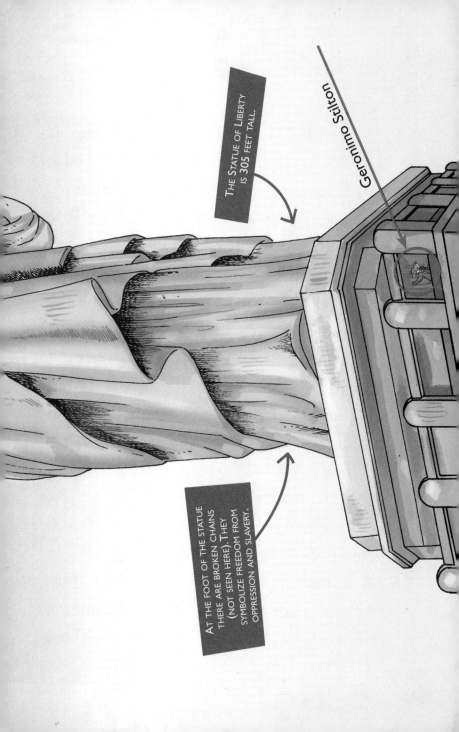

THE STATUE OF LIBERTY IS 305 FEET TALL.

Geronimo Stilton

AT THE FOOT OF THE STATUE THERE ARE BROKEN CHAINS (NOT SEEN HERE). THEY SYMBOLIZE FREEDOM FROM OPPRESSION AND SLAVERY.

When I finished cleaning, the deck was as **SHINY** as the top of another famouse New York monument, the Chrysler Building. The captain must have been pleased because he gave me a friendly pat on the back — and almost dislocated my shoulder! "This is **AMERICA**, young man! Go! Climb the statue and look to your **FUTURE**!"

I decided to follow his advice. I **DISEMBARKED** and headed toward the statue. She was even more beautiful close up.

With the **yellow** bag in tow, I got in line for the elevator that would take me up the base of the statue to Lady Liberty's feet. And holey cheese was the line long!

It seemed like every rodent in New York City was in line with me. I would be waiting for hours to get an **ELEVATOR** to the top! Without my gold pocket watch, I had no idea what time it was.

"E-e-excuse me, do you have the time?" I asked the rodent standing behind me.

"It's three thirty," she replied. **Moldy mozzarella**! Mrs. Smith had probably come and gone. I let out a squeak of **FRUSTRATION**. Would I ever see my bag again? There was only one way to find out. I had to make it to Central Park by 4 P.M.!

CENTRAL PARK

I can't begin to tell you what I had to do to get back to Manhattan. First I had to **scrub** the deck of the ferry again. Then I slogged along through the wet, **HEAVY** snow. My paws were so sore, they looked like they'd gone through a **cheese** grater.

I paused on a street corner to catch my breath. I was so tired I had to use the yellow suitcase to support myself.

A sanitation worker took pity on me and offered me a **RIDE** uptown on the back of his garbage truck.

I couldn't afford to be choosy, so I pinched my nose and scurried on board. **What a stench!** I got to Central Park on time, but I **SMELLED** like a garbage can!

I had to find Mrs. Smith here, I just had to. Then I'd finally be able to go to the MacMouses' apartment and relax. I started daydreaming about how my **RELATIVES** would *happily* welcome me . . . I'd take a nice **HOT BUBBLE BATH** . . . I'd

CENTRAL PARK

Central Park was the first landscaped park in the United States. It was designed by Frederick Law Olmsted and Calvert Vaux in 1857. The park measures 843 acres and has more than 500,000 trees and shrubs, amid its rocky outcroppings, hills, lakes, and meadows.

eat some delicious, **warm** food.

Unfortunately, I was so busy daydreaming, I forgot to look where I was going. Before you could say "visions of cheese puffs," I was trampled by a group of **RUNNERS**.

As they stomped on my aching tail, I heard them say,

"Who's that?"

"What's he doing blocking the **ROAD** like that?"

"You can tell he's not a New Yorker!"

I was too weary and numb to feel a thing. My last thought was, "Holey cheese, New Yorkers are tough! They jog in the **snow**!"

Then, for the second time that day, I fainted.

ON THE STREETS OF NEW YORK

When I came to, I was all alone. It was getting dark. The paths in Central Park were deserted. I had lost my **LAST** chance to find Mrs. Smith.

Dejected, depressed, and despondent, I *AIMLESSLY WANDERED* the streets of New York. The city looked like a *fairyland*, with Christmas lights everywhere *twinkling* against a blanket of new snow.

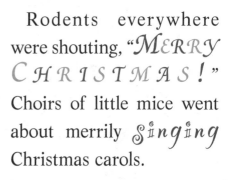

FIFTH AVENUE

GRAND CENTRAL TERMINAL

THE BRONX

Rodents everywhere were shouting, "*MERRY CHRISTMAS!*" Choirs of little mice went about merrily *singing* Christmas carols.

Jingle bells! Jingle bells...

It seemed like there was a rodent dressed as **santa claus** on every corner. They rang bells and bellowed,

86

"Merry Christmas! Happy holidays to all!"

Everybody was happy.

EVERYBODY EXCEPT ME.

Everyone was hurrying home to celebrate with their families.

EVERYBODY EXCEPT ME.

Everybody had a place to go.

EVERYBODY EXCEPT ME.

I'd never felt lonelier in my life.

I found myself at a beautiful circle with a **HUGE** statue of Columbus at its center. At that moment, an idea struck me like a *lightning* bolt.

AN IDEA!

COLUMB . . . ?

With new **hope**, I took out Mrs. A. Smith's appointment book. I looked closer at the last appointment, the one my tear had e-r-a-s-e-d.

What did "Columb" mean? I'd thought it must mean Columbia University . . . but, it could also mean **COLUMBUS CIRCLE**, one of the most famouse landmarks in Manhattan!

I looked around, trying to get my bearings.

Yes, this was Columbus Circle! It was one of the corners of Central Park!

It suddenly dawned on me that the **MacMouses** lived on Columbus Circle! I couldn't remember the address, but I remembered what the building looked like.

I'd seen it in a **photo** Grandfather William had shown me.

I still hated the idea of confessing my **mistake** to Grandfather William. But fate had brought me right to him. So what choice did I have? The only thing to do was to find the MacMouses' building and ask for help.

I walked around and around Columbus Circle until I **finally** recognized the MacMouses' building. It was an enormouse SKYSCRAPER gleaming with shiny mirrors, glass doors, and brightly lit windows.

Timid as a mouse, I pushed open the door. As it swung open, A GUST OF WARM WIND enveloped me. It felt so good to be in a warm place!

The doormouse, a TALL and **muscular** rat, was dressed in a fancy red uniform with gold epaulets on his shoulders. With an air of superiority, he stuck his snout in my face and asked, "**WHO ARE YOU?**"

I could hardly blame him for being so scornful. I was bedraggled. I **smelled** like a garbage truck. But I tried to maintain my dignity nonetheless. "I'm a **GUEST** of the MacMouses."

He stared at my soggy fur, my mud-soaked clothes, the dirty bag, and the glint of **desperation** in my eyes. Then he snorted. "Yeah, right! The likes of you a **guest** of the MacMouses!"

I tried pleading with him. "Please, would you let the MacMouses know I am here? My name is Stilton, *Geronimo Stilton*. I come from **New Mouse City**."

"Geronimo **WHO**?" he said disdainfully.
"**WHERE'S** New Mouse City? I've never
heard of it."

"My name is Stilton, *Geronimo
Stilton*," I said firmly. "I'm the publisher
of *The Rodent's Gazette*, the most famouse
newspaper on Mouse Island!"

The doormouse laughed *so* *hard* he
almost popped the shiny buttons off his
uniform. "You're kidding! You, the publisher
of a newspaper? Then I'm the president of
the United States!"

I took out my soggy business card. The
writing was still readable, though barely.

"Would you please buzz the MacMouses
for me?" I asked him. "Thank you."

He still looked suspicious, but he
BUZZED the MacMouses. "There's a
scruffy rodent here who says he's Geronimo

The Rodent's Gazette

GERONIMO STILTON

Publisher

17 Swiss Cheese Center
New Mouse City

Stilton from New Mouse City. He says you've been expecting him, but . . ."

There was a pause, and then the doormouse's expression changed from scorn to **SHOCK**. "You've really been expecting him? Really?" he asked. He looked me up and down in amazement. "Well in that case, of course."

The doormouse hung up the phone, then halfheartedly took his cap off and bowed. "Mr. Stilton, this way please. Take the **elevator** to the thirty-fourth floor."

MRS. A. SMITH

I **dragged** myself and the yellow bag to the elevator. I no longer cared that I'd lost the gifts. Not even the prospect of facing my grandfather **bothered** me. All I cared about now was taking a nice, long bubble bath and stuffing some cheese in my snout, not necessarily in that order.

I **pressed** the button for the thirty-fourth floor. While the elevator was going UP, I started thinking about what I'd say to the MacMouses and my grandfather.

Finally, the elevator door opened.

I found myself in an **IMMENSE** room decorated with elegant furniture and brightly colored Christmas decorations. It was filled with lots of SMILING rodents,

Among the many **happy** faces was my grandfather.

I threw myself on my knees before him. "Grandfather, please forgive me. I lost the bag with all the MacMouses' gifts."

My grandfather opened his mouth to squeak, but before he could say a word, someone interrupted him. "What do you mean?" a pleasant-sounding voice asked. "The gifts are right here!"

A friendly looking young rodent came toward me. She was carrying a yellow bag **JUST LIKE THE ONE** I still had clutched in my paw. Attached to the bag's handle was a bright blue tag that said _Geronimo Stilton_.

It was **MY** suitcase!

"It's . . . it's . . . it's . . ." I **STUTTERED**. "Cheesecake! Are you Mrs. A. Smith?"

The rodent **laughed**. "Yes, I'm

GERONIMO'S
SUITCASE

Mrs. A. Smith. And you're Geronimo Stilton, right?"

I was almost struck speechless. "Yes, I am Stilton, *Geronimo Stilton*," I finally answered.

"What are you doing at the MacMouses' House?"

"I'm Annabelle MacMouse Smith, Klondyke MacMouse's daughter," she explained. "I married COCONUT SMITH."

A SMILING rodent with dark fur approached and shook my paw.

"Hi, I'm Coconut Smith, Annabelle's husband! Welcome, Geronimo. We've been waiting for you since this morning."

I WAS FLABBERGASTED! "I don't understand! What do you mean you've been waiting for me since this morning?"

My grandfather cut in, "Still daydreaming, Grandson, huh? Wake up and smell the cheddar! My friend Klondyke's daughter arrived home this morning, opened that SUITCASE, and found it was not hers. But I recognized it immediately: It was your bag! Annabelle tried CALLING YOU to tell you to come immediately to COLUMBUS CIRCLE!"

I couldn't **believe** it! All day long I'd been thinking I'd never find A. Smith, that Smith was too COMMON a name, and she'd been under my snout the whole time!

"Too bad the phone battery went dead and you never got the `full message`," my grandfather went on. "We've been **WAITING** for you all day! You got here just in time for Christmas Eve **dinner**."

"But . . . but . . . your APPºᵢNᵀMᵉNᵗ book had you going some place different every hour. Why was your schedule so packed?" I asked Annabelle.

She smiled. "I thought I'd take you around **NEW YORK** and show you some of the most interesting sights. But it looks like you've already done that by yourself!"

I guess I had! I wouldn't necessarily recommend my way to other tourists, but I'd certainly **SEEN** the city from top to bottom. And now that I was nice and warm and with *family and friends* again, I could almost laugh about it. Almost.

It certainly had been an adventure!

MERRY CHRISTMAS TO ALL!

While the Stiltons and the MacMouses were celebrating Christmas, I gazed out the enormouse picture WINDOW overlooking Central Park. The snow-covered trees seemed to go on forever. It was a magical sight.

Fluffy flakes danced through the air and settled gently on the newly fallen SNOW. Those snowflakes reminded me of home. The snow that fell on NEW YORK was the same as the snow falling over New Mouse City. It just goes to show the things that really matter are the SAME everywhere. All over the world, the heart of every mouse asks for the same thing: happiness.

I turned back toward the rodents in the

Geronimo Stilton

room. There was nothing that could make me **happier** than I was at this moment, with my family and friends around me.

Stretching out my arms, I called out, "MERRY CHRISTMAS to all of you!" I turned to the MacMouses. "Thank you for including us in your holiday celebration! It's wonderful to make such marvelous new friends." Then I turned to my family.

"And it's fabumouse to be back with my family. It wouldn't be Christmas if we couldn't all be together today. I love you all!"

My sister and Benjamin rushed over and gave me a big hug. Even my grandfather came over to EMBRACE me.

Holey cheese, this was turning out to be one of the **best** Christmases ever!

Lots of Ideas to Make Your Christmas Bright

Decorate your house,
bake gingerbread cookies,
and more!

Gingerbread cookies
to decorate your christmas tree!

INGREDIENTS:

* ½ cup butter
* ½ cup granulated sugar
* 1 large egg
* ⅓ cup molasses
* 3 cups all-purpose flour
* 1 tablespoon ground ginger
* 1 tablespoon ground cinnamon
* ½ teaspoon ground nutmeg

* ¼ teaspoon ground cloves
* 1 ½ teaspoons baking soda
* 1 ¼ cups confectioners' sugar
* 1 tablespoon powdered egg white (see note)
* 2 tablespoons water
* Few drops fresh lemon juice
* Pinch of salt

Note: If you can't find powdered egg white, just make a mix of confectioners' sugar and water for the frosting. It will take a little longer to dry, but it will still taste great!

1 Place the butter, sugar, egg, and molasses in a bowl. Using a mixer or a wooden spoon, beat them until they are smooth and creamy.

2 In another bowl, combine the flour, sugar, spices, and baking soda. Then gradually mix the dry ingredients into the butter mixture. Stir until the dough is smooth.

3 Divide the dough in half and wrap each half in plastic wrap. Refrigerate for two hours.

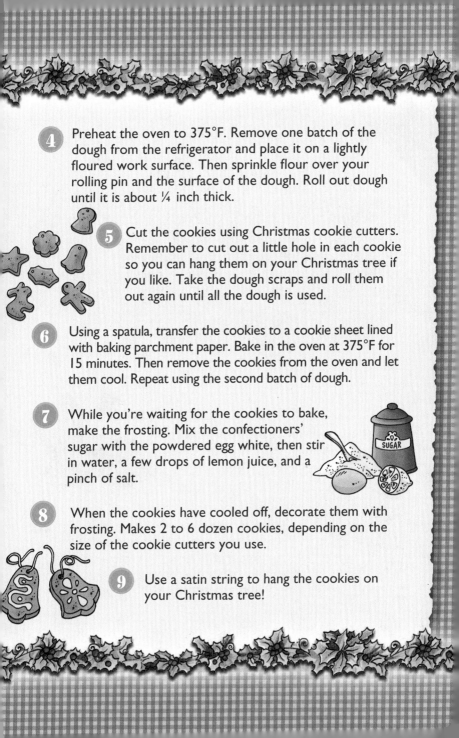

4 Preheat the oven to 375°F. Remove one batch of the dough from the refrigerator and place it on a lightly floured work surface. Then sprinkle flour over your rolling pin and the surface of the dough. Roll out dough until it is about ¼ inch thick.

5 Cut the cookies using Christmas cookie cutters. Remember to cut out a little hole in each cookie so you can hang them on your Christmas tree if you like. Take the dough scraps and roll them out again until all the dough is used.

6 Using a spatula, transfer the cookies to a cookie sheet lined with baking parchment paper. Bake in the oven at 375°F for 15 minutes. Then remove the cookies from the oven and let them cool. Repeat using the second batch of dough.

7 While you're waiting for the cookies to bake, make the frosting. Mix the confectioners' sugar with the powdered egg white, then stir in water, a few drops of lemon juice, and a pinch of salt.

8 When the cookies have cooled off, decorate them with frosting. Makes 2 to 6 dozen cookies, depending on the size of the cookie cutters you use.

9 Use a satin string to hang the cookies on your Christmas tree!

Colorful Christmas Wreaths

* A Styrofoam ring (approximately 10 inches in diameter)
* Lightweight red and green fabric
* Gold ribbon (approximately 3 inches wide)
* Plaid ribbon or any ribbon in Christmas colors
* Scissors
* One crochet hook
* One felt-tip pen

1 Cut several square pieces of red and green fabric. Each square should be approximately 2 inches by 2 inches.

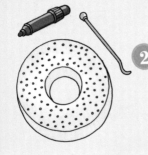

2 With a felt-tip pen, mark a series of dots approximately ½ inch apart all over the Styrofoam ring. At every dot, poke a hole with the crochet hook.

3 Place a square of the red fabric on the table. Put the tip of the crochet hook in the center of the square.

4 Fold the square around the crochet needle and, holding it firmly with your finger, push it into one of the holes.

5 Repeat this process by alternating green and red pieces of fabric. Every so often, insert a piece of the gold ribbon. Do this until the entire wreath is covered with the fabric and ribbon.

6 Once the entire wreath is covered, make a large bow with the plaid ribbon and put it on the top of the wreath. Ta-da! You're done.

Brownies

INGREDIENTS:

* ½ cup butter, plus additional melted butter for greasing pan
* 1 cup semisweet chocolate chips
* 4 large eggs
* 1 cup granulated sugar
* 1 ½ teaspoons vanilla extract
* ⅔ cup all-purpose flour
* 2 tablespoons unsweetened cocoa powder
* Confectioners' sugar for dusting brownies

1 Preheat the oven to 325°F. Grease a 9 x 9 x 2-inch baking pan with melted butter.

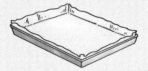

2 On your stovetop, take a heavy saucepan and melt the chocolate and butter over low heat. Then stir gently to blend well, set it aside, and let it cool.

3 Beat together the eggs, sugar, and vanilla extract. Add the melted chocolate and butter. Fold in the flour and the cocoa, and stir the mixture until it is well blended and smooth.

4 Pour the batter into the pan and spread it to the edges. Bake for 40 minutes or until the center of the top is almost firm and a toothpick inserted in the center comes out with dry crumbs sticking to it.

5 Remove the pan and let it stand for 45 minutes or until completely cool. Dust with confectioners' sugar and cut into 1½ x 3-inch bars. Makes 18 bars. Now eat up!

Want to read my next adventure?
It's sure to be a fur-raising experience!

GERONIMO'S
VALENTINE

I'll admit it: I'm a bit of a cheesy mouse. What can I say? I'm a romantic! That's why I love Valentine's Day. This year I had a date with a very special rodent—Petunia Pretty Paws! But then my private investigator friend, Hercule Poirat, called. He needed my help solving a mystery. Now I had to help Hercule AND impress Petunia at the same time. Holey cheese, what was a gentlemouse to do?

And don't miss any of my other fabumouse adventures!

#1 LOST TREASURE OF THE EMERALD EYE

#2 THE CURSE OF THE CHEESE PYRAMID

#3 CAT AND MOUSE IN A HAUNTED HOUSE

#4 I'M TOO FOND OF MY FUR!

#5 FOUR MICE DEEP IN THE JUNGLE

#6 PAWS OFF, CHEDDARFACE!

#7 RED PIZZAS FOR A BLUE COUNT

#8 ATTACK OF THE BANDIT CATS

#9 A FABUMOUSE VACATION FOR GERONIMO

#10 ALL BECAUSE OF A CUP OF COFFEE

#11 IT'S HALLOWEEN, YOU 'FRAIDY MOUSE!

#12 MERRY CHRISTMAS, GERONIMO!

#13 THE PHANTOM OF THE SUBWAY

#14 THE TEMPLE OF THE RUBY OF FIRE

#15 THE MONA MOUSA CODE

#16 A CHEESE-COLORED CAMPER

#17 WATCH YOUR WHISKERS, STILTON!

#18 SHIPWRECK ON THE PIRATE ISLANDS

#19 MY NAME IS STILTON, GERONIMO STILTON

#20 SURF'S UP, GERONIMO!

#21 THE WILD, WILD WEST

#22 THE SECRET OF CACKLEFUR CASTLE

A CHRISTMAS TALE

#23 VALENTINE'S DAY DISASTER

#24 FIELD TRIP TO NIAGARA FALLS

#25 THE SEARCH FOR SUNKEN TREASURE

#26 THE MUMMY WITH NO NAME

#27 THE CHRISTMAS TOY FACTORY

#28 WEDDING CRASHER

#29 DOWN AND OUT DOWN UNDER

#30 THE MOUSE ISLAND MARATHON

#31 THE MYSTERIOUS CHEESE THIEF

CHRISTMAS CATASTROPHE

#32 VALLEY OF THE GIANT SKELETONS

#33 GERONIMO AND THE GOLD MEDAL MYSTERY

#34 GERONIMO STILTON, SECRET AGENT

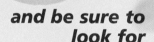

and be sure to look for

#36 GERONIMO'S VALENTINE

ABOUT THE AUTHOR

Born in New Mouse City, Mouse Island, Geronimo Stilton is Rattus Emeritus of Mousomorphic Literature and of Neo-Ratonic Comparative Philosophy. For the past twenty years, he has been running *The Rodent's Gazette,* New Mouse City's most widely read daily newspaper.

Stilton was awarded the Ratitzer Prize for his scoops on *The Curse of the Cheese Pyramid* and *The Search for Sunken Treasure.* He has also received the Andersen 2000 Prize for Personality of the Year. One of his bestsellers won the 2002 eBook Award for world's best ratlings' electronic book. His works have been published all over the globe.

In his spare time, Mr. Stilton collects antique cheese rinds and plays golf. But what he most enjoys is telling stories to his nephew Benjamin.

THE RODENT'S GAZETTE

1. Main entrance
2. Printing presses (where the books and newspaper are printed)
3. Accounts department
4. Editorial room (where the editors, illustrators, and designers work)
5. Geronimo Stilton's office
6. Storage space for Geronimo's books

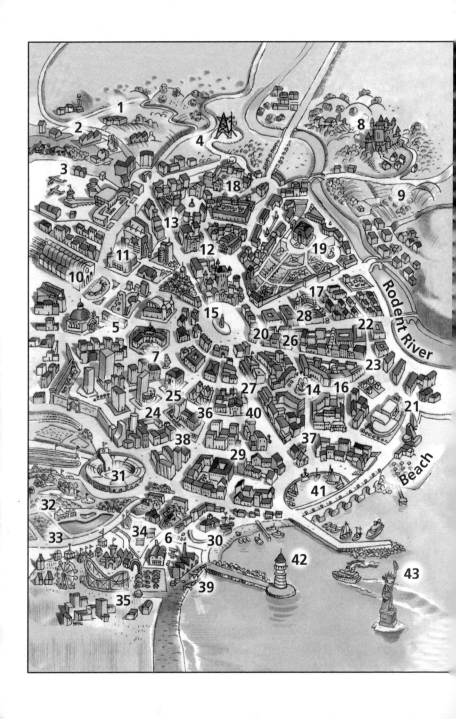

Map of New Mouse City

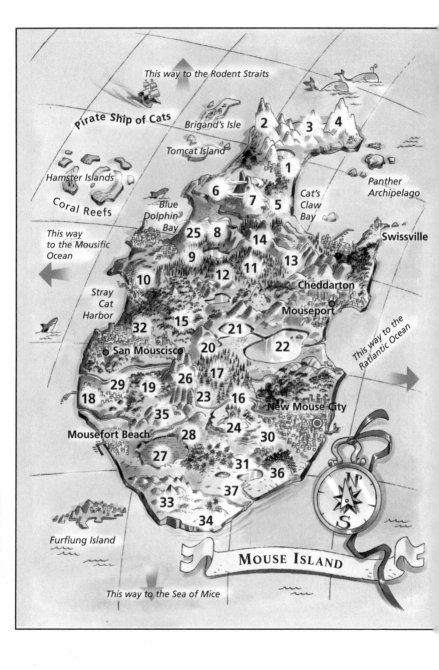

This way to the Rodent Straits

Pirate Ship of Cats

Brigand's Isle

Tomcat Island

Hamster Islands

Coral Reefs

Blue Dolphin Bay

This way to the Mousific Ocean

Stray Cat Harbor

Cat's Claw Bay

Panther Archipelago

Swissville

Cheddarton

Mouseport

This way to the Ratlantic Ocean

San Mouscisco

New Mouse City

Mousefort Beach

Furflung Island

MOUSE ISLAND

This way to the Sea of Mice

Map of Mouse Island

1. Big Ice Lake
2. Frozen Fur Peak
3. Slipperyslopes Glacier
4. Coldcreeps Peak
5. Ratzikistan
6. Transratania
7. Mount Vamp
8. Roastedrat Volcano
9. Brimstone Lake
10. Poopedcat Pass
11. Stinko Peak
12. Dark Forest
13. Vain Vampires Valley
14. Goose Bumps Gorge
15. The Shadow Line Pass
16. Penny Pincher Castle
17. Nature Reserve Park
18. Las Ratayas Marinas
19. Fossil Forest
20. Lake Lake
21. Lake Lakelake
22. Lake Lakelakelake
23. Cheddar Crag
24. Cannycat Castle
25. Valley of the Giant Sequoia
26. Cheddar Springs
27. Sulfurous Swamp
28. Old Reliable Geyser
29. Vole Vale
30. Ravingrat Ravine
31. Gnat Marshes
32. Munster Highlands
33. Mousehara Desert
34. Oasis of the Sweaty Camel
35. Cabbagehead Hill
36. Rattytrap Jungle
37. Rio Mosquito

Dear mouse friends,
Thanks for reading, and farewell
till the next book.
It'll be another whisker-licking-good
adventure, and that's a promise!

Geronimo Stilton